Charles and Melinda

ANGELA DELOIS BUTLER

America Star Books
Frederick, Maryland

Softcover 9781682298039

PUBLISHED BY AMERICA STAR BOOKS, LLLP

www.americastarbooks.pub

Frederick, Maryland

TABLE OF CONTENTS

CHAPTER 1
Charles and Laura

In the month of March, 1926, a son was born to Charles and Laura. That son was named after his father. Charles and Laura absolutely loved and adored all their children. Charles Jr. was their eighth, and they later added two more babies to their family.

Even though Charles and Laura were former slaves, but their children were not. Because slavery ended in 1865, and Charles's father and mother had received their forty acres and a mule. Nevertheless, it was still not uncommon for African-Americans to have their children taken from them, especially in the Deep South.

Charles Jr. was born to parents who were once slaves, parents who knew hardship. In 1933, when Charles was only seven, their debtor a (white man), who claimed they owed money for merchandise, that Charles Sr. had bought from his store decided to sell him to another sharecropper who owned a different land and fields. During the sharecropper era in the United States, blacks had to work off their debt to their owners. Under the Jim Crow law, his parents allowed the white store owner, to trade their son to work and pay off their families debt or could claim that the slaves owed for merchandise, forcing them to make some sort of payment arrangements. Usually, this debt was paid with sweat, hard work and labor performed by the black people who allegedly owed something to someone. Because during that time era there was debtor's prison, for those who did not want to work off their debts.

Charles's new white debtor was named Jacob Scott, and he was different from other slave owners, in that he didn't overexert his slaves, and he was known for feeding his sharecroppers well. He rarely split up families, and he made sure they had more than one set of clothes for each season, as well as suitable shoes. Also, he wasn't one to use the whip.

It was a hard time for African-Americans, even after slavery was abolished, because the children of former slaves were still often treated like slaves, all under the guise of sharecropping, especially in the 1920s and 1930s. Nevertheless, Charles always dreamt of being truly free. Even though Charles was a child, the laws of the era prevented him from being able to go to school. This law only applied to those children who were working off debts.

Charles grew up to be a tall man, and even though he could not read or write, he learned to count with the help of his brothers and sisters. He did not see his family often, but he did become one of Mr. Johnson's favorites. s this right? I ask because in the next few paragraphs, you mention a Mr. Johnson often treated them like slaves, especially in the In time, he was placed as a head over the other sharecroppers. That meant he no longer had to pick cotton or other crops.

Eventually, Charles began to be paid wages. He bought some property with the money he earned, and he hired others to plant and pick on halves. He even managed to pay them, even though he could only sign his name with an "X." Charles's siblings could read and write and had an understanding of mathematics. As a family, they began to purchase land of their own.

As mentioned previously, Charles's father was one of the few black men who actually received his forty acres and a mule after slavery ended, so that gave the family a nice start too. Unfortunately, when the Ku Klux Klan (KKK) learned that they were ready to harvest their fields, they paid the family a visit. The first time they came was in the dead of night, and it was pitch black outside, other than the bright, orange, burning light of a cross that had been set on fire. The family knew the hooded ones would be back. They knew the cross was a warning, telling them, "Leave or die," but they wanted to fight for their hard-earned land. Fueled by deep anger rather than fear, they loaded their guns and gathered up any axes and tools that could do harm.

Charles's family waited into the late hours, listening for the racist intruders. As they expected, the KKK showed up the very next night, but they were surprised when bullets started flying at them. Charles and his family knew their every inch of their property and knew exactly where to place themselves so they had the advantage. The Klan was unaware of the ditches and other hiding places on their property. When the KKK realized they were defeated, they left the property and did not return. The Ku Klux Klan members could be heard saying loudly "those crazy nigga's or trying to kill us!!! They's a know we are white men, we white!!! than add they left the property. Than add Charles said to his family "They will be back but not too soon!!! But all that a matters is that they are gone.

Charles and his family continued to buy land, separately and together, and before it was all said and done, they owned hundreds of acres of land, and they knew how to protect it.

CHAPTER 2
Melinda

Melinda was born in October of 1928, the sixth child of Melissa. In all, Melissa had a dozen children, none of them from the same father. Because this was considered taboo and a disgrace, the other women in Melissa's community constantly talked about them, and her children were frequently ostracized by adults and kids alike. Melinda had tried to question her mother (when she was younger) about her night time men visitors but was told, 'yuse a child!! youse stays in a chiles place, you hear"? Melinda was educated and attended school, along with her siblings, but she was not immune to the cruelty of her classmates; she felt the stares and heard the whispers and jeers coming from the other young people. She did not attend school year round, so her brother and sisters taught her what they knew, and she followed suit when they went on to become maids and sharecroppers.

Like others of her time, Melinda endured a hard life. She labored in the fields in the blazing sun in the summer and froze in the winter. As sharecroppers, her family lived on the white people's land and toiled and labored hard, but they were seldom paid. Many times, there was not enough food to go around, so her parents often went without. Melissa labored hard and made up the difference in her children's absence from sun up to sundown, but they sent their children off to school, determined that they would be educated. After school, the children toiled right by their side. The white children went to school all year but the black children did not go to school during harvesting time.

When she was sixteen, she and three of her sisters were sent to take care of the children of the land owner. Those children were very different from Melinda and her sisters, for they were well dressed and had no calluses on their white hands. In addition to childcare, Melinda was also tasked with cooking and cleaning for the family. As the sharecroppers' family grew and her younger sisters became older, they all took care of their owners grandchildren and helped to farm the land, working in the fields whenever they were told, trying to earn their food and a place to stay.

Melinda was always astounded at the size of the owner's home. Compared to what she called "the big house," her family's accommodations were very small and meager. With permission, she and her sisters often took the leftovers from the plates of the owner's family so they could share it with their mother and their younger siblings.

As Melinda grew older, she took an interest in learning and understanding more about the Bible. Her faith grew with every church service she attended, and her spiritual life was very important to her. Her entire family went to church, and it touched each of them differently.

By the age of twenty-two, Melinda knew she wanted a different life than the one she and others like her were living. Church and spirituals were very much a way of life for her and her family, and they were a great comfort for Melinda. She often sang in the church choir and loved to praise the Lord, expressing herself through songs. The spirituals they sang in the choir echoed the suffering of them and their ancestors, but still they loved to lift their voices to praise God for the hope He offered them.

Every year, an annual gospel revival was held at one of the nearby churches, to be attended from people from miles around.

Melinda was very excited when the event was scheduled to be held at the church she was a member of, for she knew it meant meeting new people and seeing some they had not seen for over a year.

As the family pumped water to fill their washtubs, then ironed their clothes and prepared their hair for the following day, Melinda did not know that that particular Sunday would mark the beginning of a week that would forever change her life.

CHAPTER 3
Sweet Revival Surprise

Charles was not a very religious man. He liked to drink, though not in excess, and he had always thought church was boring. As a child, he was forced to go, and if he dared to fall asleep during the sermon, it earned him a pinch of his ear. As an adult, his family could seldom ever persuade him to go.

When he was twenty-four, he heard about the week-long gospel event coming to the area. His brothers and sisters could not stop excitedly chattering about all the friends they would see again, and his sisters mentioned that several young men would be there. As much as he despised sitting through long church services, something about the revival piqued his interest. Out of respect for the church, he deliberately avoided drinking anything on Saturday, and the next morning, he put on his Sunday best and smoothed and brushed his hair.

That Sunday morning, Charles and his family loaded up in two cars; Charles drove a white Chevrolet 150, and the other vehicle was a Chevrolet 20. It was rare for blacks to own cars in the 1950s, so the cars were definitely considered luxury items for a family such as his. As a matter of fact, Charles's family were the only blacks within a sixty-mile radius who owned cars.

Meanwhile, Melinda and her family walked the short distance from their home to their church. She was so happy to be in the house of the Lord, and she proudly sang out the spiritual, words that had meant so much to her ancestors before her. The songs and hymns had been carried down from the 1800s, and as she sang those lyrics, Melinda could almost picture the slaves in her head, singing to uplift themselves in a time when there was no freedom available to them. She felt their pain, but she also heard the joy of knowing about Heaven. In those songs, she found the calm assurance that all of their torment would be over someday.

Charles glanced around at the people in the congregation, and a young woman caught his eye. She was short but had a nice figure. He couldn't help but admire the way she shouted and praised God with the other women in the church. As the preacher spoke about a new day and the power of God, Charles continued to watch the lady, hoping to catch a glimpse of the young woman's face. Throughout the duration of the service, he became very familiar with her back. Melinda was encouraged by the sermon and had high hopes for a better day, for freedom for her and for all like her. As she listened, her sister leaned over to whisper in her ear.

"One day, we'll be free…and so will our children and their children's children."

"Yes, because God is real," Melinda whispered back. Hope kept her going, a strong and enduring hope and a constant prayer for a better life.

The church was growing hotter by the minute, or so it seemed to Melinda. The temperature was even hotter because the place was packed from one wall to the other, with people filling all the pews and even the aisles. When the first pastor stopped preaching, Melinda and one of her sisters escaped outside, in search of some fresh air.

Charles continued looking around at the crowd. He knew some of the folks, but there were many who were strangers to him. He often found his eyes resting on the backside of a certain young woman, even though he could not see her face. Finally, as he was idly looking around, the object of his interest stood, turned, and walked quickly down the aisle, giving her a full view of her beautiful face and attractive figure. He left the pew to follow her, with his brother in tow.

"Whew. It sure is hot in there," Melinda said, fanning her face and trying to cool off. "All those people in there!"

As she finished her last sentence, she felt as if she was being watched. She looked around uneasily, and, sure enough, saw a man staring at her from behind a tree, not too far off. Melinda quickly turned her head away from him and said to her sister, "See that tall man, to the right? He's staring right at me. Don't look yet. Just turn slightly and glance."

"The one in the blue?" Maxine asked.

"Yes, him."

"He's walkin' our way," Maxine said.

When Charles and his brother walked up to them, Charles introduced himself right away. "Hello. My name is Charles, and this is my brother, Nathan."

"Hello," Melinda and her sister said together, then told the young men their names.

"Nice to meet you, Melinda and Maxine," Charles politely said.

When it was time to go back inside the church, the four decided to stay outdoors to get to know each other better.

"I'm twenty-four," Charles said. "I'm not married, and I don't have any children."

"Same here," Melinda said.

"Did you walk here?" Maxine asked.

"No. We have cars. I drove Nathan's Chevy 150," Charles answered. He then went on to talk to Melinda about his family and where he lived. "I farm my own land," he explained, "and my family farms each other's properties. We also farm the land our mama and daddy left us." Melinda told Charles that she was twenty-two, that she still lived at home, and that she worked as a maid and sharecropper. "We don't own any property," she said, "but I work with twelve other men and women, including the two butlers from the big house. Sometimes we have to work the fields. There are about 100 sharecroppers in all."

She went on to tell Charles about her strong faith and her belief in God. "I believe He will deliver me and all our people," she said resolutely. "I don't understand why whites are the way they are or why things are the way they are, but I pray frequently, and I believe He'll answer my prayers one day."

As Melinda listened to Charles, she began to take a real liking to his strong Southern voice; it reminded her of the bass singers in the choir. For some reason, right from the first moment she met him, she felt safe. When the rest of her family and his exited the church for the evening, she felt disappointed that the night was coming to an end.

"I'll see you again tomorrow night, won't I?" Charles asked Melinda.

"The revival lasts a week, and I'll be here every night," she said, smiling sweetly.

"I will be here tomorrow night also. After all, I can't go wrong hearing about God."

Melinda and her family walked the short walk back home. As they walked, her thoughts kept returning to Charles. She loved that he seemed so straightforward, as that was a quality she'd always admired in a man. She did not understand what she felt or why, but she had never felt that way about any many before. The feeling was far different from her usual feelings about men, including the other sharecroppers and their sons. She had been around men her whole life, and she wasn't uneasy or intimidated by them, but there was truly something special about Charles. Several men had expressed interest in her, but she had never felt that strange fluttering in her stomach when she was with him. Now, whenever Charles crossed her mind, her stomach did flip-flops and her palms grew sweaty.

The one thing that really nagged her about Charles was that he could not read, including her mother Melissa. She wondered if he even wanted to learn. Many black people were illiterate in those days, and, just like Charles, they could only sign their name with an "X." She also wondered how he knew the Bible so well, since he obviously could not read the words on the pages of the Good Book. *Maybe he memorized the scriptures and just recites them,* she thought. The other thing she could not figure out was how he had managed to acquire so much land, as well as cars. *He must be fibbing, just to make himself look good,* she finally convinced herself.

The following day, Melinda and her sisters went about their work at the big house. Melinda was in the hot kitchen, with sweat pouring for her face and neck as she chopped vegetables, readied the meats, and cooked along with the other servants of the big house. While she worked, Melinda's mind began to drift. She had always been quite the dreamer, and she imagined herself all dressed up, like the whites always were at their fancy dinners. She pictured herself practically floating down the stairs in a beautiful gown. She continued fantasizing and daydreaming, until the head chef snapped her back to reality. "Get on out to the fields," she said. "Maybe then you'll appreciate your job in here and start payin' attention to what you're doing."

In the hot field, she continued thinking about Charles. While many of the people she knew could not read or write, she wanted to teach him if he was willing to learn.

The day progressed, the sun started to go down, and Melinda gladly left the field and went home, where her family was all getting ready to go to the revival meeting. They pumped well water, and each one took a turn to bathe in the big silver washtub.

At the revival, Melinda looked for Charles, but she could not find him among the crowd, so she hurried to the empty seat her family had saved for her. As the visiting choir sang a beautiful and powerful rendition of "Amazing Grace," Melinda began to feel better, as if her soul and mind were being renewed. She had a feeling that life was going to get much better for her and her loved ones. Just as the pastor began to preach, she felt a gentle touch on her sleeve.

"May we join you?" Charles quietly asked.

Melinda and her family quickly made room for him and his brother Nathan.

"To God, one day is like a thousand years," the preacher said from the pulpit. "God is patience. He is love. As the children of God, we should be patient, as was the Lord. God wanted His people to be longsuffering, and that God heard the cries of His people. God does not count time as we do. That God would not allow His children to suffer for much longer. God Himself would wipe away every tear from their eyes!" He went on to quote much scripture and talked about the love of God and how he sent Jesus to die for them.

As the church took a break to allow another choir and preacher to take his place, Melinda and Maxine again went outside to get some fresh air. Again, Charles and Nathan followed them, but this time, Charles escorted Melinda to his car and opened the door for her. Little did she know that he had already decided that she would someday be his wife.

Charles and Melinda really got to know each other during the week of revival. When the seven-day gospel event ended, Charles promised to visit Melinda, and she agreed to see him also. They said their goodbyes, and Melinda went back to her everyday life, not expecting to ever see him again.

CHAPTER 4
A Better Life

While Melinda doubted that she would ever see Charles again, she did pray and ask God if he was the one for her. Much to her surprise and delight, Charles kept his promise and visited three days later to take her and her sisters for a ride. Nathan was thrilled to see Maxine again, and both sisters were elated.

Melinda loved her mother dearly, but Melissa had done things that were not looked kindly upon by those in their community. The family was often shunned, even by other blacks. Even though Melinda and her family tried hard not to let it bother them and held their heads high, they often cringed inside at the gossip and all the bad things that were said about them and their mother. In spite of all that, Charles did not stop visiting her, nor did he judge Melinda by her mother's past. He was a great listener, and he often brought food for Melinda and her family.

Three months later, Melinda was pleasantly surprised when he gave her a ring and asked her to marry him. She had never expected that anyone would propose to her, especially because of all the talk and her mother's reputation, even though Melinda herself was a virgin. When she expressed her shock to Charles, he simply said, "You are not your mother."

Charles was not alone in his proposal, for his brother Nathan also proposed to Maxine. Both young men got down on one knee, and they even properly asked Melissa for her daughters' hands in marriage. Melissa was happy to give her blessing, knowing that her girls would have a good life with Charles and Nathan and that they would always remain close as both sisters and sisters-in-law. Melinda and her sister decided to marry on the very same day, and they were excited about jumping the broom at their double-wedding, an old African tradition from their motherland.

As the wedding approached, Melinda was so excited she could barely work. Fortunately, for once, the head maid and head cook let her slide, especially since she was invited to the wedding.

It was important for Charles, Melinda, Nathan, and Maxine to incorporate traditional African elements in their American wedding ceremony. Both couples agreed that they would jump the broom. Melissa planned to wear a white dress, but it would be adorned with red and accessories, including a headpiece and shoes to complement the African attire. Her sister would wear a similar garment, only accented with blue. The guests would consist of mostly relatives and church members. Charles and Nathan were happy to furnish food, as they had raised plenty of livestock and crops on their farms.

A week before her wedding day, Melinda grew nervous. She wondered what her first night as Charles's wife would be like. She was a virgin, and her curiosity soon turned into fear, so she spoke to her mother about it.

"It will be fine," her mother reassured her. "It's not as bad as you think, especially if he loves you."

"But I don't know anything about what happens after the marriage, Mama," Melinda said.

Melissa wrapped an arm around her and smiled. "That's a good thing. That way, he'll have proof that he is your first. You will have plenty to eat and will never go hungry, because he has his own vast lands to farm. That is a blessing in itself."

"I will never forget you or my family, Mama," Melinda said. "I will make sure you don't go hungry."

Her mother smiled again and said, "I believe you will, and I have prayed for a better life for all of you."

Melinda was not the only would-be bride suffering from a bad case of pre-wedding jitters, for her sister Maxine was a bundle of nerves as well, and she also sought reassurance from her mother and family. Maxine was told the same thing as Melinda by their mother. Maxine said to Melinda, "Who's more nervous, me or you?"

"I'm not sure, but I'll be glad when this is all over with," Melinda answered.

Maxine readily agreed as they hung wet clothes on the line. "This is what I want," she said, "but I just wish I knew more."

"Knew more? About what?"

"About his life," Maxine said. "I mean, I know they are farmers, but I wonder if they are as nice as they seem, his family. Ya know?"

"We just have to be ourselves," Melinda said. "We cannot ever be someone else. Either they'll love us or they won't.'"

"You're right about that!"

Charles and his family brought food and clothes for Melinda's family twice a week, and she could truly say she'd never been hungry since she'd met him. And that Melinda and Melissa debt was paid in full by Charles and Nathan. The cruelty of being a sharecropper, maid, and cook did not always guarantee that she had food or money, because the people who lived in the big house and owned the land did not always do right by the hardworking people who toiled away for them. There were many families like Melinda's, but she didn't like focusing too much on the bad and the sad.

One thing that continued to bother her was that Charles was not as religious as her. He seemed to love God, but he did not necessarily believe the Bible, even though he knew a lot of

God's Word by heart. Charles did not believe every word that was written in the Bible. He often asked Melinda, "Why would the devil want to give us hope of better"? They gave us blacks the Bible but these same people made our people slaves. And us, we are nothing to whites but second class "niggas". I do know there is a God but...some of that about slaves obey their masters...is wrong. My parents were slaves and I live in segregation and everyone I know. Jim Crow is a living hell for me,you, and all people who look like us". I believe that whites are evil even though my family owns and farms land. And Melinda could only say, "God will change everything we just have to pray and believe in him". She wasn't sure if that would cause a problem between them, but she certainly hoped it wouldn't. God was very important to her, an everyday part of her life, and she wasn't about to give Him up.

There were always rumors about an uprising or takeover, but none ever happened where Melinda lived. She wanted a better life, but she also longed to be truly free. She did not feel that it was God's will for people like her to go without necessities like food, no matter where they came from or what color their skin was. The people in the big house had plenty to spare, but she felt in her heart and mind that God loved her just as much as He loved people of other races.

She feared the armed white men who protected the 400 acres of farmland she worked on, but she was thankful that they were eventually allowed to leave. After many years, they could ultimately pay off their debt for food and clothing. Other blacks she knew were not so fortunate; they only way they could leave was through the sweet escape of death. Knowing that there were worse conditions to deal with was what kept many where they were, including her family.

Melinda didn't want much beyond common needs and a few creature comforts. She dreamt of nice clothes and decent shelter, a house that stayed warm in the winter and didn't have a leaky roof. She wanted and prayed for a better life, and she felt she was entitled to the same things as Caucasians, especially since she and other black people seemed to do all the hard work for them. They even breast-fed their babies so the fine white ladies could get their womanly figures back more quickly.

Lynchings happened, even if they were only talked about behind closed doors, and Melinda and her family understood what they could and could not do. They knew the limits, the boundaries, and the rules, and they hoped that keeping them would prevent them from being lynched. There were "Whites Only" signs everywhere, and the bathrooms reserved for blacks were filled with maggots. She did not dare go out at certain times, so as to avoid being raped, lynched, or both. In spite of her approaching marriage and the fact that she loved Charles and knew he loved her, she still had what her mother called "itching ears and feet." She often wanted to leave or run away but she stayed. She did not like feeling like a slave; even though it had been outlawed in 1865, she still felt like one. Knowing that it would only end when the white man's heart changed, she prayed often for change. Specifically, Melinda prayed for a complete end to the Jim Crow laws, not only for her benefit but also for the benefit and freedom of everyone she knew. She had great faith and the patience the preacher had talked about at the revival, and she knew change would only come when God was good and ready.

Melinda continued to see Charles, and her love and respect for her fiancé and his for her seemed to grow more and more with each passing day. Sometimes they took long walks with Nathan and Maxine, though the couples often went their own direction for a little privacy. They found great joy and laughter in just being together, and the best part was that they knew they had a lifetime to love each other. Charles and Nathan were not ever bothered by the white men who guarded the property because he had permission from their boss and also Melinda knew of other ways to come onto the property. Charles was never seen by the whites in his wagons, as the whites seldom ever visited the place where the black couples lived, so they were free to simply enjoy their time together. It was indeed a beautiful, wonderful time in the lives of those young couples, and they learned about each other, loved one another, and remained the best of friends.

CHAPTER 5
Weddings Day

On the day of the weddings, right at dawn, Melinda woke up and looked around, knowing it would probably be her last morning in that small house where she'd spent so much of her life. In spite of the leaky roof, the lack of indoor plumbing that forced her to have to go out to the smelly outhouse to do her business, and the cold winters, she would miss the tiny house. She would also miss her mother and her siblings. She felt a little sad, as she would greatly miss the chatter and laughter of her family. Some of them were already working at the big house, but they had permission to take off early for the special day.

Her sister Maxine had already bathed and was straightening her hair with the hot comb. When Maxine saw Melinda, she immediately placed the hot comb in the fireplace embers. "Good morning, Melinda," she said.

"Good morning. You beat me up this morning."

"Yes, I've been up a while. I already ironed my clothes with Mother CC's iron," she said, referring to their next-door neighbor who was always letting them borrow things. "Wasn't it nice of her to loan us her iron and board?"

"Yes, very," Melinda said, smiling. "Well, it's my turn to get ready now, I guess." She then looked at her beautiful sister seriously. "Are you scared, Maxine?"

"Not anymore. I prayed to God and left everything in His hands."

"Me too," Melinda said. "I have to."

Melinda's mother was a bony woman, so large that she had trouble getting around. She hugged Melinda with her big arms, laughed, and said, "You'll both be just fine. I's a-believin' for ya both."

"I believe also, Mama," Melinda said, hugging her back.

Melinda ironed her clothes and put the hot comb through her hair, with her sister's help. They always assisted one another with that, and they laughed a lot as they did so.

Once both the brides were ready to go, most of the family rode in a borrowed wagon, but some rode with Melissa and Melinda once the wagons were off the property. As they rode along, for the first time in a long time, Melinda began to feel that everything was going to be all right. Just like her sister had, she decided to place all her trust in God and leave it there with Him.

Melinda and Maxine arrived with their family before Charles and Nathan got there. *This is it,* Melinda thought as she looked at the massive oak tree their ceremony would be held under. *I'm about to be married.*

Within a couple hours, everyone had gathered for the ceremony. When Melinda finally spotted Charles, she was so happy; a deep sense of love stirred within her when her eyes fell on him and he caught her gaze and looked lovingly back at her.

Soon, both brides were standing before their pastor, with their soon-to-be husbands. Drums began to beat, and the traditional African dance begin in honor of their African ancestors. Melissa and Melinda danced before their husbands in time to the fast and slow tempo of the drums. As the songs became louder, everyone's feet moved faster.

Melinda was almost in a daze when she heard her pastor tell them to jump the broom. She felt Charles grab her hand,

and they jumped over one broom while Maxine and Nathan jumped over another. Just like that, they were man and wife and man and wife. The marriages were legal, by way of an American wedding license, but they had made sure to pay honor and tribute to their African roots in the ceremony itself, much to the delight of all in attendance.

The festivities continued, and food and drinks were in abundance. People laughed and danced and had a great time, dancing and clapping in tune with the drums and music from the modern record player. The wedding celebration would be one that was talked about and fondly remembered by their family and neighbors for years to come.

* * *

The day after the wedding, Melinda awoke in her new home. It was a wooden house with four rooms, stocked with plenty of food, which was the part Melinda loved most of all. As she looked around at the new life she'd been given, she thought of her less fortunate family and asked Charles if he would continue to help them.

"Yes, of course. They're now my family also," he said.

Charles walked with Melinda around the property and told her all about his dreams. He had high hopes of employing other blacks and allowing them to earn pay by picking on halves and delivering the crops to others and collecting money from them. Even though the majority of them at that time were his on family including extended family. Which included cousins also and now Melinda's family. In other words, they could take half of what they picked to keep for themselves or to sell.

"You're so smart, Charles," Melinda told him, and she immediately agreed to work alongside him to help him make his dreams come true.

CHAPTER 6
The First Ten Years

As she promised, Melinda worked right beside her husband and his crew, planting and gathering the crops. She worked hard, just as the others did, and she was grateful for her marriage and the new life she'd been given.

Before long, Melinda gave birth to her first child, Faye. She considered her daughter to be a good baby, as she slept through the night and didn't cry about being strapped to Melinda's back while she worked in the sun, in a papoose similar to what Native Americans used to use.

As little Faye grew, Melinda came to realize just how intelligent her daughter was. She learned fast and often listened to her mother quietly. She learned to speak quickly and did not complain like her cousins, Maxine's children, often did. Melinda's second baby, Jacklyn, also caught on fast and was never a complainer, which made her mother very proud.

* * *

Charles's dream eventually became a reality. In 1956, though, he was confronted by the vicious Ku Klux Klan, who had decided they wanted part of the money he made. The red faced white man spit tobacco and said to Charles, "Pretty wive you have a there, would hate for anything to happen to er". Yep pretty that one is, nice, real nice, all that you a havein' here. Charles blood boiled and it took every thing in him not to kill the white man standing before him. But he looked at his axe and felt the sweat run down his face from his labor. The sun was so hot but he did not raise his axe but looked around him at the other white men. He than said while clinching the axe, "How much do you wants"? Charles felt he had no choice but to agree to their demands, but by two years later, he had had enough of the bed sheet-wearers digging into his pockets to take his hard-earned money. "I am tired of this," he told Melinda. "It's my money. Why should I share? We worked for this, not them." He then told his wife that he had no intention of giving another cent of his money away.

"Have you lost your mind?"

"Yes," he answered firmly, "and for the better."

Melinda pleaded with Charles, but it did no good.

* * *

Faye continued to help her father count his part of the money, but two or three times, Charles was short. Faye being a child did not understand everything but understood that her father was being cheated by the whites.

"He owes me a lot, Faye," Charles said.

Having no idea what her father meant, she only smiled.

"Do what?"

"They are cheating me out of my half."

"Well, God will work it out. You'll see," Melinda tried to reassure him.

"When?"

As strong as her faith was, Melinda had no answer for him.

About a week later, Charles talked to Melinda again, so bitter and panicked that he made her cry. "We will not have enough to live on. What good is all our hard labor? What good is owning land? Even I know that your Bible says, 'A man should not eat if he does not labor.' What wrong have I done to deserve this? I only abided by God's law. You will not be able to sew, not even for our daughters. There will be no money to buy fabric or store-bought clothes for winter, not even for our daughters. I have decided we must go to Mississippi."

For the first time in their marriage, Melinda spoke very boldly to her husband in stern disagreement. "No! I will not go with you to Mississippi, nor will my children."

"You do not have a choice. I chose to keep all the money, and they will come for us."

Having no choice, Melinda packed up as much as she could, and they fled in the dark of night, illuminated only by the burning of two crosses and their own home on fire. Melinda refused to look back, and when they boarded the bus, they quietly ushered themselves to the very back and left the front for the whites, as they still had to abide by the Jim Crow law.

CHAPTER 7
Mississippi

Mississippi was worse than Alabama, much worse. It was common knowledge that lynchings and other horrible, horrific things were done to blacks there, right out in the open. Poor little Faye saw and understood too much for a child, but so was the way of the world during the time of the Jim Crow laws. It was not at all uncommon to see black men and women hanging by their necks from the trees that lined the red clay roads of Mississippi, often for the smallest of mistakes or wrongdoings—anything the white people deemed an insult or a crime. Jacklyn was too young to understand, but Faye was not. Murder was often committed on those back country roads, and Melinda would never forget the moss on the trees where her people died.

Melinda tried to make the best of it for herself and her daughters. When they were not sweating and toiling away in the fields of Mississippi, she spent a lot of time educating her girls, teaching them to read, write, and to do math. She hoped that would give them a fighting chance in a world that didn't seem to want to grant them any.

Charles also realized he'd made a mistake in moving his wife and daughters to that horrendous place where racism and cruelty were running rampant. "I have relatives in Florida," he said. "I believe it will be better for us there."

Once again, hoping for a better life and a safer one, Melinda gathered their belongings and their children. Again in the dead of yet another night, Charles and Melissa boarded a bus and crept to the back with their belongings and their babies.

When they arrived in Florida, they walked the short distance to the home of Charles's kinfolk. It was dark outside, but they were welcomed by Jacob, his second cousin on his father's side. Jacob's wife, Tara, looked as if she was part-Native American, but she greeted them warmly, and Melinda helped her fix up plates for everyone.

As soon as the children were fed and put to bed, Charles had a lot to say. "I just could not take it anymore," he explained. "It was my land, my property, and they wouldn't let me keep what was mine. I know my family considers me crazy, but I just could not do it any longer. I got tired of all that 'Yes, sir' and 'No, ma'am' business, having to pay respect to the very people who were so shamelessly taking from us, stealing from us. Not only did I have to pay them, but they also cheated me out of my part. My brothers are upset. They want to fight, but what's the use? We'll never win anyway, so I just took my family and left. Believe it or not, Mississippi's worse. Every day there, someone on the sharecroppers' land was beaten or hanged. They didn't even bother to give 'em respectable burials, just left 'em hanging from the trees. I can't go back to Alabama, because I'm considered a thief there. That's why I'm here."

His cousin Jacob shook his head. "It ain't much better here, but the hanging and beatings are not nearly as bad. They're going to be lookin' for you though. If they're scared enough, someone might tell 'em where you ran off to."

"Yeah, I know," Charles said, "but what's done is done."

"You can stay here till you find someplace else. These white folks 'round here are always looking for people to keep up their yards and businesses, but some of them still take taxes out."

"We pay taxes and still get cheated," Charles said. "It's not fair, but I guess it's the law."

"Times are changing," Jacob encouraged. "You didn't see it 'cause you were in the deep, deep parts of Mississippi, but they're a-marchin', trying to change things for us colored folks. It's 1955, and a lot's been going on. They're carrying signs and everything, and in some places, there have even been sit-ins, at businesses and such."

Charles eyed widened. "Is that right?" he asked in disbelief. "Well now…"

Jacob went on to say, "They's a-callin' for equality for all, including us colored folks. We work just as hard but have to go to the back. That ain't right. Those theater balconies are hot and unclean."

"It sounds good," Charles said, "but I don't believe them whites will ever accept us as equals. They hate us, kill us, steal from us. How will that ever change? They'll only find new ways to do it."

As the night turned into morning, the four black people talked and reminisced about the old days, when they were young. All of their lives had been hard, with much suffering, but they took some comfort in the fact that they didn't have to struggle through it alone. They had their God, and they had each other.

* * *

Jacob and Charles went walking, in the hopes of finding a job for Charles. Six hours later, Charles was employed to do yard work and fix up equipment at a business. He would work for ten to twelve hours a day and would be paid daily.

A few days later, Tara told Melinda all about her cleaning jobs. She informed her of who would and would not pay colored people, which whites in their community took pity on them. "The missus of that house on the hill would rather die than pay hardly anything at all. She's in her seventies, and she doesn't believe in paying coloreds," she said. "You have to work for food, somethin' I found out the hard way."

"I sure appreciate you's a-tellin' me this," Melinda said.

"The missus on the other side of the hill needs a maid. She'll work you real hard, but she pays. Your back might feel like it's breaking, but she's good about paying her maids. She might even let you take your children with you. You can ask her. I work for that missus also."

"When can we go ask her?" Melinda said.

"Sunrise tomorrow."

CHAPTER 8
Hope

True to her word, Tara awoke and took Melinda along with her to her job. "Be quiet," she warned Melinda. "The mister and missus ain't awake this early."

Melinda helped Tara sweep the long porches that wrapped all the way around the big house, almost in a complete circle. After the first floor was swept entirely, breakfast was prepared.

Tara respectively waited for the family of four to seat themselves, then said to the missus, "She's here, the girl I told you about, the one who is lookin' for work."

"Let me see her," the missus replied.

"Yes, ma'am," Melinda said, quickly stepping forward.

"You're not lazy, are you?" the missus asked.

Melinda shook her head. "No, ma'am. I'm not scared of work."

The woman seemed satisfied with her answer and quickly gave her a onceover. "I will pay you three dollars a day and no more."

"Yes, ma'am," Melinda quickly replied. "I understand."

"Also, I cannot stand a thief. I will not tolerate anyone stealing from me."

"I will never take anything that ain't rightfully mine," Melinda assured her.

"All right. I'll give you two dollars for today and three dollars every day hereafter. Do you understand?"

"Yes, ma'am."

As they worked throughout the rest of the day, Tara told Melinda in a whisper, "Ya know, that missus is real bad about leaving money lyin' around."

Melinda worked very hard, just as she had done with her sisters at the big house before. She tried not to think about the past too much, to remember all that she and Charles had left behind in Alabama, but sometimes she could not help but think about her family. Still, she had great hope for a better future. *God willing, things will work out,* she told herself over and over again. She'd lived through pain and suffering, and hard work and struggling were familiar to her. *But as for freedom? Not yet, but I still got hope,* she thought.

CHAPTER 9
Chain Gang

As time went on, Melinda and Charles began to breathe a little easier. They found another place to live, and their children seemed to sleep better once they were on their own instead of all crammed up with Jacob and Tara. Both of them worked hard, long hours, but they had plenty of food, and things seemed to be working out for them.

After a while, Charles grew homesick and wanted to see his family, so he decided they would make a trip back to Alabama. It was a good trip, and Charles felt like he was home.

On the way back, as they set on the back of the bus, Melinda begin to relax, relieved that they had not been caught by the KKK. When they left the bus station back in Florida, all of them on foot, they had to walk past a group of white people, who refused to step out of their way and give them a clear walking path. Their oldest child, Faye, was forced to walk in smoldering cigar butts that were still orange and smoking on the end, and her feet were badly burned. She tried her best to be a brave little girl, but she couldn't stop the tears from rolling down her cheeks as her mother and father tried to doctor her feet. Charles and Melinda felt helpless, but Charles knew there would be horrendous consequences if he tried to fight back, so he had to hold his peace.

Over time, Charles began to have a drinking problem, and he was often found in a drunken slumber after work. Melinda did her best to console him and tell him that things would get better someday, but the Jim Crow laws could not be ignored, and they affected their lives each and every day, everywhere they went.

* * *

Their worst fear was realized when the white man Charles supposedly stole from found him and brought up charges against him. Charles was shackled to nine others and walked behind them. As he boarded the bus, he tried hard not to show the hatred he felt, as he knew lashing out would only get him in worse trouble. Charles knew he had made a mistake going back to Alabama. They had made it out and had not been recognized while leaving the first time. But someone told on them and where they lived but he refused to think about what that person went through, who told.

The black men on the chain gang were forced to work on the railroads in the rain, cold, and heat. Charles lost weight, but he no longer cared. They were fed three times a day, but the meals were meager, and since Charles wasn't even sure what kind of grub he was being fed, he often refused to eat it. He felt defeated, angry, and beaten down, but he did have family to visit, and that kept him going.

As the years passed, Charles's hair whitened, and his hands became cracked and blistered from so many long days of hard work. He knew he would be free one day, but he had no idea when that day would come. The prisoners were made to pick the vegetable fields, and since cotton was king in the South, where all the money was made, Charles, along with hundreds of blacks, also had to pick cotton for hours on end. The incarcerated, guilty or innocent, were a perfect source of forced free labor, and the prison system was quick to put them to work on any tasks that had to be done.

There were women in prison, too, but they were usually separated from the men. They all picked cotton and labored long, hard hours, with no concern about the weather or the toll it might take on their weary bodies. Pregnant women were given only a little leeway, but the wardens and prison staff had a hard time dealing with them. When there was no one on the outside to claim the children, the inmates were left to care for them. Desperate to free their children, the young mothers often smothered their babies, to keep them from having to grow up in the prison system. Those children who did survive were usually kept in prison until they were old enough to labor with their mothers, but no matter how hard they tried, the guards could not prevent all the mothers from killing their newborns. Some of the infants didn't live to breathe their first breath due to miscarriage or disease, but in some way, that was sometimes a blessing. In the eyes of those mothers and all prisoners, death was better than life in prison, and they wanted to give their children that one bit of mercy something they never had. They wanted to set them free.

CHAPTER 10
What's in a Name?

As the oldest of Charles and Melinda's children, Faye wanted to know the most. One day, she asked her mother a question: "Mom, why do the white ladies call us 'girl'?"

Melinda looked at her daughter in surprise and answered, "I did not realize you noticed that."

"Mama, you said your name is Melinda. Why don't they call you by name?"

Melinda stopped washing clothes in the big silver pot, then walked three steps away and sat down. "Names are very important, but some people do not see us as equals, honey," she said to her daughter. "We know we are people like them, but they do not see us the same way. I've been called 'girl' all my life. I don't believe the people I work for even know my name or yours. Still, you must always tell yourself something important."

"What, Mama?"

"God knows your name, and so do the angels in Heaven. It does not matter what people call you. It's about what you call yourself. You might be called 'girl' all your life, but you're still a child of God."

Faye then asked, "But when do I become a woman?"

Melinda looked deep in her daughter's brown eyes and said, "You may not ever be a woman to them, but you are a woman, just like Eve, in the Holy Bible."

Faye, still not satisfied, asked, "When do the boys at school become men? They're sometimes called different names too. Aren't their real names important?"

"They have names as well, but the whites sometimes call them other things. They will grow into men, like your father, when they get older."

"But they call Mr. Gary 'boy,' and he's almost ninety years old," Faye argued.

"God sees Mr. Gary as a man created in His image," Melinda said, "but in these times…Well, that's just what they call him."

"Is my father going to be called a man or 'Charles' or 'boy'?"

"No matter what they call him, you must still respect and love him," Melinda said. "You should do the same for all people, no matter what color they are. That includes Mr. Gary."

"I will be a woman one day, and I will be called Ms. Faye,"
Melinda averted her eyes. "And if they don't?"

"I will tell them that's my name," said Faye.

"Maybe one day, but not now. I do not want you to feel the missus's belt lashes. You must never expect whites to refer to you as 'miss' or by your name."

"I understand," Faye said. "I don't want no whippings." Of course, she said that only to satisfy her mother, for she had no intention of letting a white woman beat her. She did not care about the whites not liking her, because she did not really like them either.

Faye missed her father a lot and thought about and prayed for him often. She just knew her father would not agree with her mother. As the years passed, Faye began to understand her mother's point of view, especially when she would look down the road waiting on her father to come home and give her a piggy back ride. But before long Faye was too old and big for piggy back rides, so she stopped looking for him but when someone spat on her, she spat back, and if anyone hit her, she hit back, much to her stunned mother's dismay.

That is how Charles used to be, Melinda thought, recalling her husband's defiance toward the whites who had stolen his money. She realized that their little girl, Faye, had inherited his spirit. She was afraid for Faye, but she was secretly glad that her daughter would not take any abuse from anyone.

* * *

Time waned on, and after seven years, Charles and many others were set free. He immediately went back to Florida. When he boarded the bus, he sat in the front, something he'd never done before. The year was 1964, and racial segregation had, for the most part, come to an end.

As soon as he got off the bus, Melinda and his children were there to greet him. Charles noticed the hard calluses on Melinda's hands. She was thinner, and he could see that she'd been working very, very hard.

When they returned home, he was happy to see that his wife had prepared a delicious meal for him. After he ate, he had a long talk with his daughters, who were older now and both in school. He knew it would take time for them to get to know him, but to his surprise, they were not afraid to hug him and cling to him, and he felt the love the girls still had for their father.

Faye and Jacklyn were now attending an integrated school, and neither one really liked going. They told their father that others spat on them and that they'd been attacked by dogs and their classmates. Faye was a straight-A student, but she was not being given her hard-earned high marks and was only graded with B's and C's. Before integration, she'd been valedictorian of her class.

Faye voiced her confusion to her father. "I have never been this close to whites. They look a lot different than me. They also act different. I think they're part-cat, with all those funny-colored eyes."

Charles looked into the eyes of his oldest daughter and said, "You just go to school and do something with your life. God will handle the rest." He then looked over at his wife and noticed the lines etched in her pretty face. He knew it had been very hard for his wife, but he smiled back at her when she managed to smile at him.

Melinda caught Charles up on the Civil Rights Movement, things that had changed while he was in prison. He already knew about some things but not all of them. He was very impressed with the public transportation and the boycotts, and he was finally proud of his people for standing up for equality.

Charles went on about his life, and he learned that much had change in the South, especially concerning public segregation. The "Whites Only" signs were gone. The clothes were different, and coloreds now called themselves "blacks." Things had changed, and life had gone on without him. The one thing that had not changed was his love for Melinda and his two girls. Melinda still looked at him with love in her eyes, and he adored her. Even Jim Crow could not stop love and family, no matter how hard they tried. When he looked at his wife, he still saw her as that lovely young woman he'd fallen in love with at that church revival so long ago.

CHAPTER 11
Change

For the very first time, Charles experienced eating in a restaurant alongside whites. He was a bit uncertain at first, but his friend assured him that it would be all right. When he walked in, some people looked at him with hate-filled stares, but no harm was done to either of them. As time went on, Charles decided that the whites still hated them, but they somehow managed to contain that hatred.

At home, Charles told his wife, "Their hearts and minds have not changed. They still hate blacks. I wonder how long will it be before they are unable to hide what's really still going on in their hearts."

Melinda had no answer, so she remained quiet.

As time passed, Charles's words rang true. Within two months after his release, another arrest was made, the first arrest in the area since segregation had ended. It was an arrest the whites seemed to celebrate, for a young black male by the name of Joshua was picked up for supposedly hitting a white man in a squabble over his pay for the week, which he claimed was short. Whether he actually hit the man or not was uncertain, but after he went to jail, no one ever saw or heard from young Joshua again.

"Their hearts have not changed," Charles said to his cousin Jacob. "They will always hate us."

Despite the bad, though, Melinda and Charles determinedly kept their marriage together. They attended church regularly as a family, and Melinda begin to teach her husband to read. Charles was resistant at first, but he wanted to be able to read the Bible for himself.

Melinda was overjoyed to be able to teach him. She started off with the alphabet. Much like their daughters, Charles was a fast learner, and it did not take long before he was able to sign his own name and read full sentences. Melinda also taught Charles to do math. It was a plus that he could count, because that made teaching him so much easier. He learned how to do simple to complex calculations, from adding and subtracting to multiplication, algebra, and fractions. Charles was not the only one who was learning though; Faye was an excellent student, and even in a relatively hateful environment with the odds seemingly stacked against her, she continued to excel far above her peers.

"If you could do it again, would you keep the money this time?" Melinda asked her husband.

Charles replied, "You will call me crazy, but yes. That was my work, my sweat, and my land. I regret having to be away from you and the girls for so long, but I do not regret keeping what is mine."

"What about our land? What has happened to it now?" Melinda asked.

"My family has it."

"Can we go back?"

"Yes. We can go back home, Melinda. We can finally go home, back to what is ours."

With tears in her eyes and joy in her heart, Melinda cried, "Thank you, God!"

Charles smiled with joy in his own eyes and echoed, "Yes! Thank you, God!"

CHAPTER 12
Sweet Home Alabama

Charles was looking forward to returning to Alabama. No longer would he and his wife and daughters have to live among strangers; the girls would do the rest of their growing up on their own land. The most important thing to Charles was that they would be surrounded by his very large family, surrounded by love and safety. Unfortunately, Melinda could not have any more children, but that did not stop her for having lots of children around her.

Within a week, Charles and his family boarded the bus and were soon on their way home. Melinda looked out the window and smiled when the scenery began to look familiar. The barns and the growing crops sparked so many fond memories of family, as well as recollections of the sweet beginnings of her married life.

As soon as they disembarked from the bus, they were immediately surrounded by relatives, both hers and his. Their families had grown a lot in the last decade, and there were new husbands, wives, and children to meet. While the family had changed in number and faces, in their hearts, they were still the same. Charles's family had continued helping Melinda's, and her kin even lived on the land owned by Charles's. Just as the family had grown in number, their acreage had also grown; they now owned ranches, more farmland, and even some horses and stables.

Charles and Melinda would stay with Nathan and Maxine for a while, but not before eating and celebrating with their families and friends. So much had changed, yet so much had stayed the same. In Melinda's family, there had been three marriages, and there were six more children to get to know. She was happy to discover that she had new nieces and nephews. She had seen some of her relatives over the last decade but not all at one time. Her sisters' husbands all worked with her husband's family, and the fact that they had all stuck together really touched her heart.

Melinda had been afraid to go back home after the burning crosses and the burning of her home. Both families had to fight because of Charles's actions, but none of them blamed him. Some had even gone to jail. Still, there was great power in numbers, and their extended family included many cousins, aunts, and uncles, all of whom lived locally. Because they had stood strong together and due to the end of segregation in America, they were free, at least as free as they had ever been in their lives. The U.S. Army had been sent in to keep the peace, so many blacks felt safer, at least during this time period. Charles's family had even kept his car and hidden it for him, and he was happy about that, even though it was a decade old.

"Brother, you were right," Nathan said. "What good is land if you work it only to give your labor and money to someone else? They will still try to take more than their fair share, but we are united as a family and community. I see your point. I really do.

"Good, my brother. Good," Charles said, glad to hear it.

* * *

The girls basked in all the love and attention of their family, and Melinda even had a chance to watch television, a highly entertaining thing that she did not have in Florida. She had missed working with her sisters, missed all the laughter and the jokes they told, so she was happy to help them harvest crops again.

Before she went to sleep and every time she woke up, she thanked God for all he had done for them. She taught her children to do the same, and she reveled in feeling so free and safe. She knew how valuable and important freedom was, because she had spent her childhood and most of her adulthood as a sharecropper. Things were different now. She knew that, and she was thankful for it.

Since he'd learned to read, Charles could usually be found with a book in hand, usually the Bible, after his daily farming duties were done. He was pleased with himself for learning, because he enjoyed the feeling of grasping the meaning of words. The best part was that no one could ever steal that understanding and knowledge from him. Melinda continued to encourage him and their daughters to educate themselves as much as possible, because she understood what education could do for her children.

* * *

Their first year back in Alabama passed, and it was a blessed year for them all. Much to her surprise, Melinda even became pregnant and birthed a son, Daniel.

"But the doctor said I could not have any more children," Melinda said.

"Doctors don't know everything, but God does, and He blesses people as He wants," Charles said.

Daniel, much to Melinda's joy, was easy to train to sleep through the night, unless he suffered from colic, which didn't happen often. Melinda had learned a lot in rearing her girls, so she knew to keep him awake during the day. As he grew older, she strapped him to her back like an Indian squaw, just as she had done with her girls, so she could work with her husband and family. The labor was not easy, but it was worth it to them. Even though some blacks had left the South because of segregation and the hardship and inhumanness of sharecropping.

CHAPTER 13
Faye Marries

Faye, the oldest child of Charles of Melinda, met the love of her life and fell madly in love with him. That young man was named Samuel, and he chased twenty-one-year-old Melinda all the way to marriage ceremony. The happy couple jumped the broom, just as her mother and father had over two decades before. At the ceremony, they danced a traditional African dance, the same dance Faye's great-grandfather and grandmother had danced.

"My parents' marriage has lasted," Faye whispered in Daniel's ear during their dance, "and I'm sure my great-grandparents are looking down on us, laughing and smiling."

And just maybe Charles Sr., whose name he took from a pair of shoe box after the civil war and slavery ended he changed his slave name, was looking down and smiling and saying, "They's all right. Our children are free and all right. Praise God! Praise God!"

THE END